ART, STORY, LETTERS, AND COVER
MANNY GUEVARRA

ELEMENT PUBLISHING LLC

COPYRIGHT © MANNY GUEVARRA.
ALL RIGHTS RESERVED.

ORIGINALLY PUBLISHED IN WEBCOMIC FORMAT, JUNE 2022.
FIRST PRINT EDITION PUBLISHED BY ELEMENT PUBLISHING LLC,
JANUARY 2025. THIS BOOK OR ANY PORTION THEREOF MAY NOT BE
REPRODUCED OR USED IN ANY MANNER WHATSOEVER WITHOUT THE
EXPRESS WRITTEN PERMISSION OF THE PUBLISHER.
PRINT ISBN: 979-8-9918305-4-6.

Seed of Grief

Contents

PART I: THE FIRE 5

PART II: THE FLOOD 54

BONUS CHAPTER 91

NEXT VOLUME PREVIEW 109

VISUAL GLOSSARY 116

ARTWORK AND VISUAL DEVELOPMENT 120

ACKNOWLEDGEMENTS 130

YOUR MISGUIDED,

FRUITLESS,

HAS CLOUDED YOUR JUDGMENT, PRINCE GRIEVE.

BUT I HAVE FAITH IN YOU.

AND I VOW...

"IF WE JUST—"

"MY POOR, SWEET CHILD."

SLAM!

"YOUR TONGUE IS *BITTER*—"

"WITH THE POISON FROM THAT WRETCHED HEATHEN."

JOSEPH...?

YOU ARE SIMPLY HERE TO *WATCH*, PRINCE GRIEVE.

NO...

PLEASE...

"PLEASE!"

"PUNISH ME INSTEAD!"

"I BEG OF YOU, FATHER!"

"PLEASE...

LET JOSEPH GO...

THEY DIDN'T DO ANYTHING WRONG..."

"SILENCE, HEATHEN.

YOU *DIGUST* ME."

CAN'T... MOVE...
AAAAGGGHHH!
ZZZAP!
LANK
THUD
TAT
TAT
TAT
WHOOSH
RYLEY.

FATHER.

THE KNIGHT'S ESCAPE WAS THE FAULT OF MY MEN.

I TAKE FULL RESPONSIBILITY FOR THIS FOLLY,

......

BUT IT IS MY FIRM BELIEF...

"THAT MY MEN AND I CAN RE-SECURE

BOTH THE PRINCE AND HIS KNIGH—

GGGKK!

CCRRAACK!

THUD THUD

CONGRATULATIONS, ABBOT.

YOU'VE BEEN PROMOTED.

IT SEEMS THIS **FAILURE** OF AN HEIR... IS **TRULY BEYOND SAVING.**

THERE IS NO LONGER A NEED... TO KEEP HIM ALIVE.

"I *KNOW*!

BECAUSE I FEEL THE SAME EXACT WAY ABOUT *YOU!*

AND THAT'S OUR *PROBLEM*, JOSEPH!"

"PROB- PROBLEM?"

OUR "LOVE..."

HAS BEEN NOTHING BUT A **HINDRANCE!**

AN EASILY-EXPLOITABLE WEAKNESS.

"IT'S BEEN **DOOMED** FROM THE START!"

CCCRAAACK

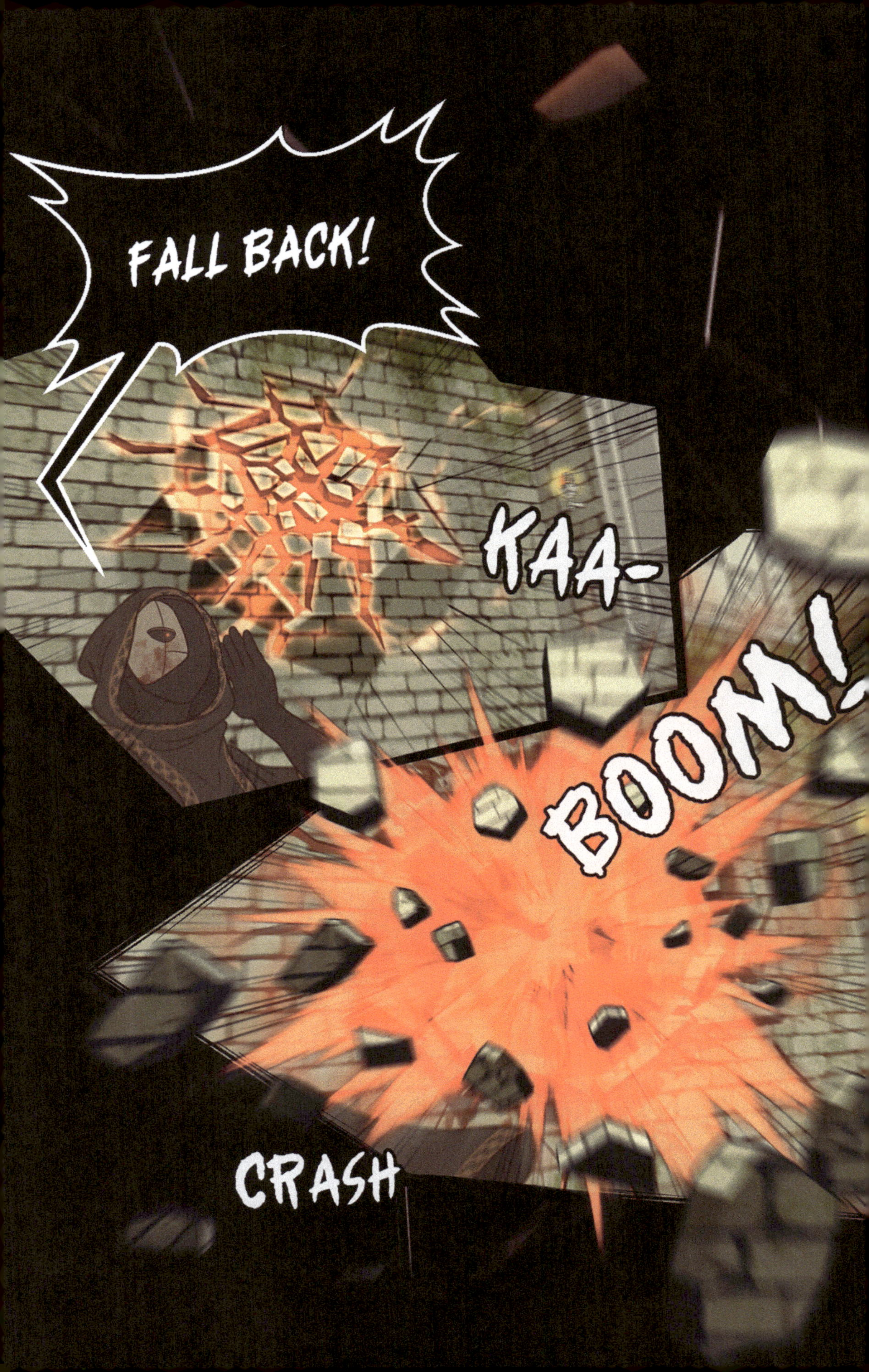
FALL BACK!
KAA-
BOOM!
CRASH

WATCH OUT!

FWOOM!

FWOOSH

"I CAN HELP YOU."

TRIP

SLAM

"I CAN *FREE* YOU FROM THIS PLACE."

RISE

"NO..."

"FROM *FATHER*."

"NO..."

"NO...!"

GRAB

DELUGE!

IS THAT...A COMMAND?

DE-LUGE.

ZZZT

DE-LUGE.

DE-LUGE.

ZZZAP!
DE-LUGE.
LOOSEN
SPLASH
SPLASH
DE-LUGE.
DE-LUGE.
SPLASH
DE-LUGE.
SLIDE
DE-LUGE.

JOSEPH.

I'M SO
SORRY.

JOSEPH,
MY KNIGHT...

JOSEPH, MY KNIGHT,

YOU ARE...

THE BEAUTIFUL SPRING OF WATER

THAT SOOTHES MY MIND.

"YES, MY PRINCE."

"YOUR LOVE..."

"IS MY GREATEST STRENGTH."

"I WILL STAY BY YOUR SIDE"

RUMBLE

THIS LOVE-

RUMBLE

BURST!

THIS **STRENGTH** THAT YOU ALL HAVE GIVEN ME-

THUD

THUD

EARTHEATERS

Seed of Grief

BONUS CHAPTER

ARTIFICER?

EARTHEATERS
WILL RETURN

Thank you to all my Kickstarter backers, Patrons, and readers over the years. Without you, this publication would not have been possible, and drawing comics would feel a lot less magical.

THAT IT SPRINGS FORTH FROM THEIR PHYSICAL FORM

POP~

AND DANCES GLEEFULLY

THROUGH THE WORLD AROUND THEM.

SEEMINGLY ASKING FOR YOUR HAND.

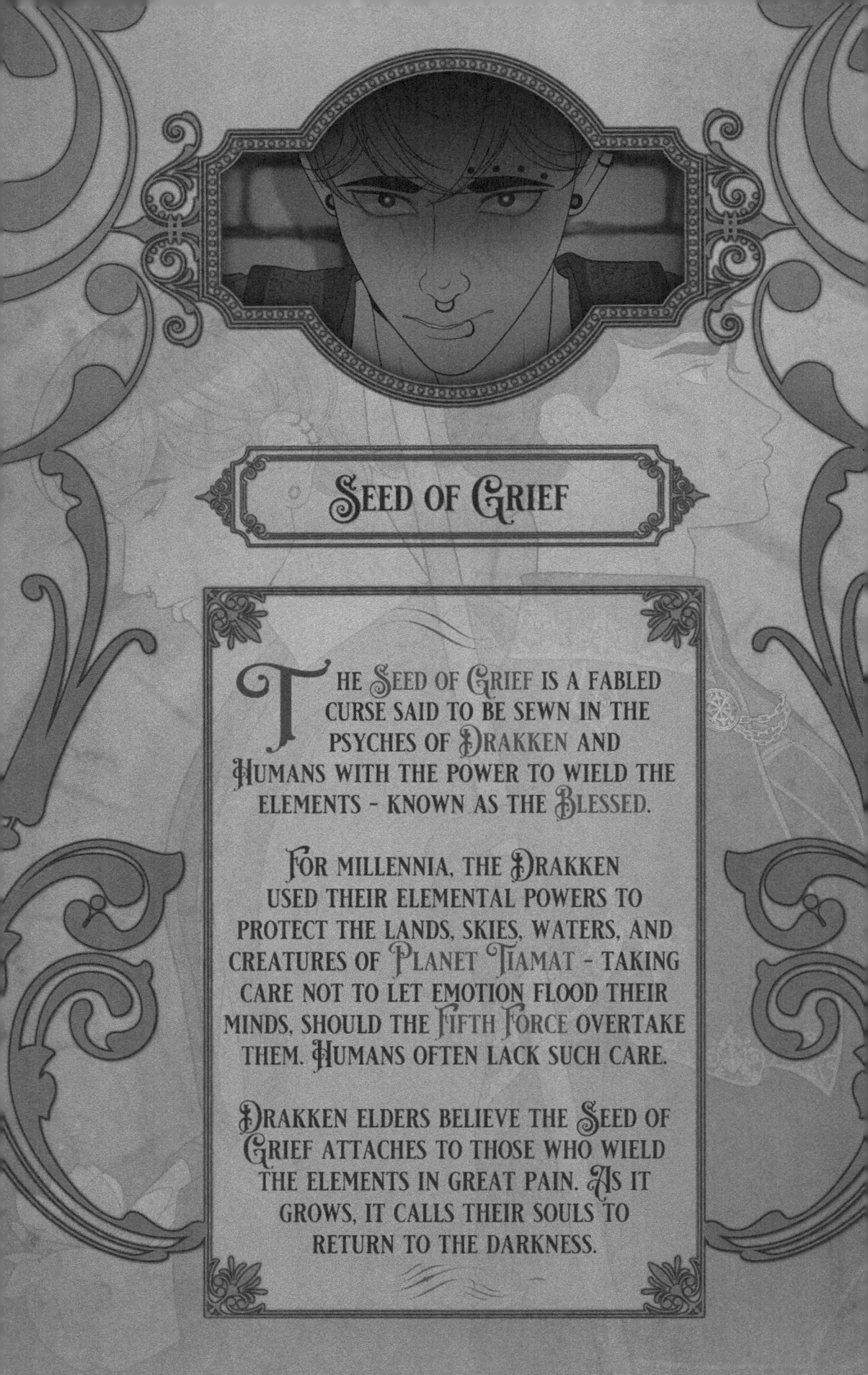

Seed of Grief

The Seed of Grief is a fabled curse said to be sewn in the psyches of Drakken and Humans with the power to wield the elements – known as the Blessed.

For millennia, the Drakken used their elemental powers to protect the lands, skies, waters, and creatures of Planet Tiamat – taking care not to let emotion flood their minds, should the Fifth Force overtake them. Humans often lack such care.

Drakken elders believe the Seed of Grief attaches to those who wield the elements in great pain. As it grows, it calls their souls to return to the darkness.

Planet Tiamat

The fifth planet from the sun in the inner system of the Milky Way Galaxy. Once thought to have been destroyed, this terrestrial super-earth lies between Mars and the gas giant Jupiter - and is very much alive, teeming with diverse life.

After Humankind's destruction of Earth, the orphaned species saught refuge on a newly-discovered Planet Tiamat, thinking it fate - only to discover Her lands to be the domain of beings much more powerful than Man: the Drakken.

These great serpents are said to have been blessed by Tiamat Herself with the power to move mountains.

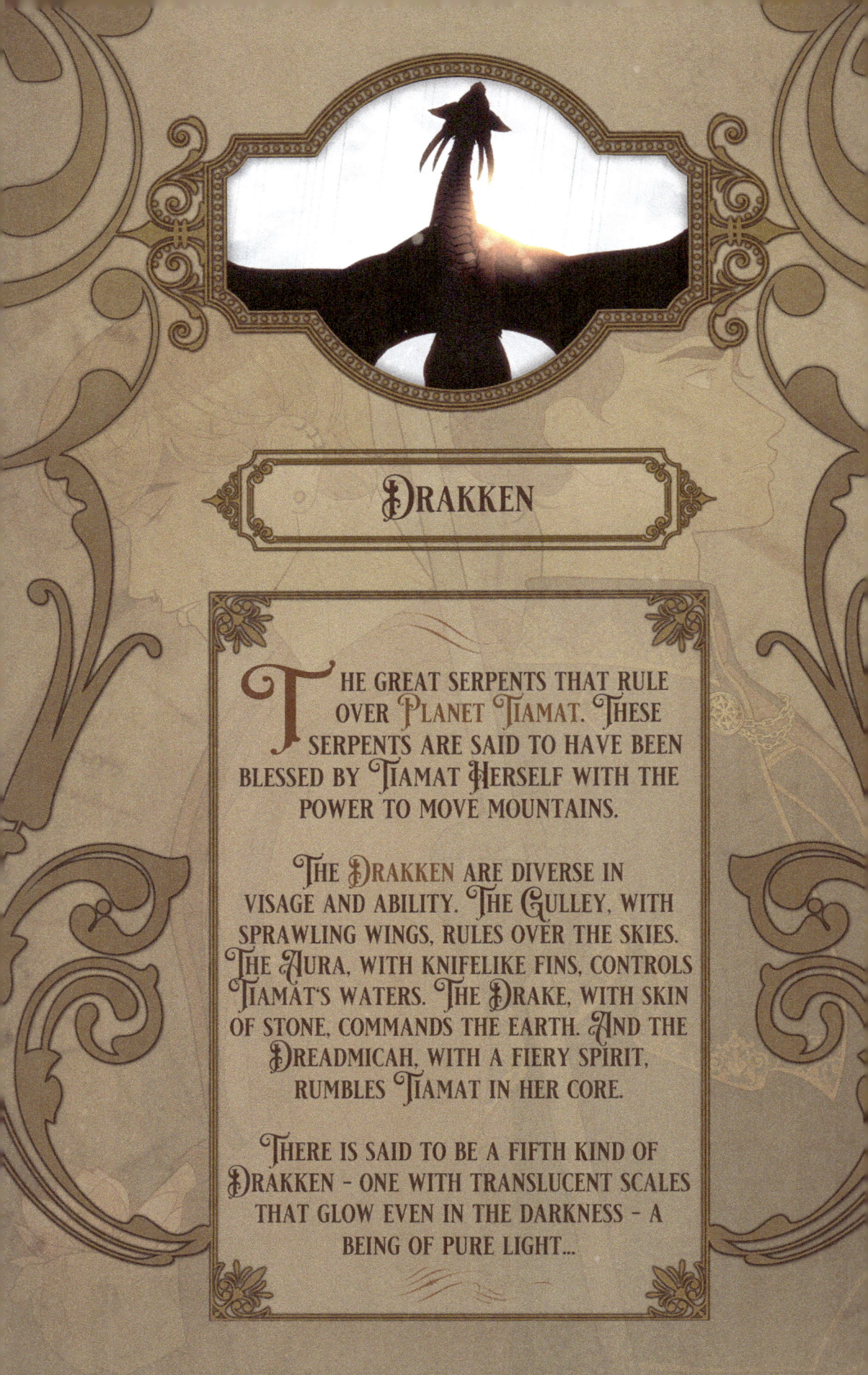

Drakken

The great serpents that rule over Planet Tiamat. These serpents are said to have been blessed by Tiamat Herself with the power to move mountains.

The Drakken are diverse in visage and ability. The Gulley, with sprawling wings, rules over the skies. The Aura, with knifelike fins, controls Tiamat's waters. The Drake, with skin of stone, commands the earth. And the Dreadmicah, with a fiery spirit, rumbles Tiamat in her core.

There is said to be a fifth kind of Drakken – one with translucent scales that glow even in the darkness – a being of pure light...

Blessed

Mighty beings that possess the power to wield the natural elements of Planet Tiamat. The Drakken, rulers of Tiamat, possess this power, known as the Fifth Force. The great serpents use these abilities to protect the lands, skies, waters, and creatures of the planet.

Drakken elders say that these elemental powers were bestowed upon the first Drakken millennia ago by the Goddess of Tiamat Herself. As such, the Drakken are hailed as demigods by the native creatures of Tiamat, blessed with the power to move mountains.

When Humankind arrived on Planet Tiamat, they were not expecting to meet their match.

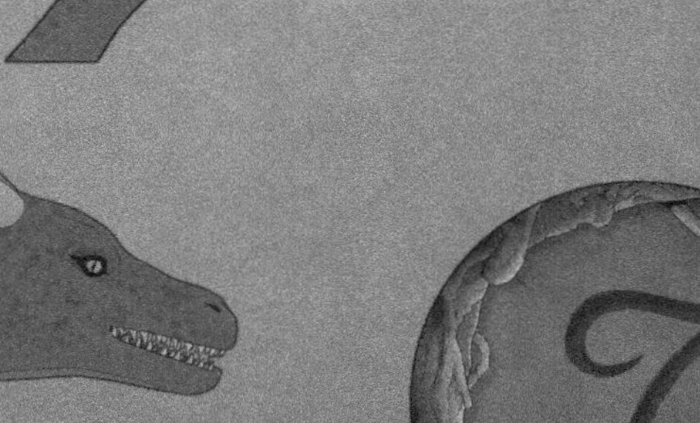

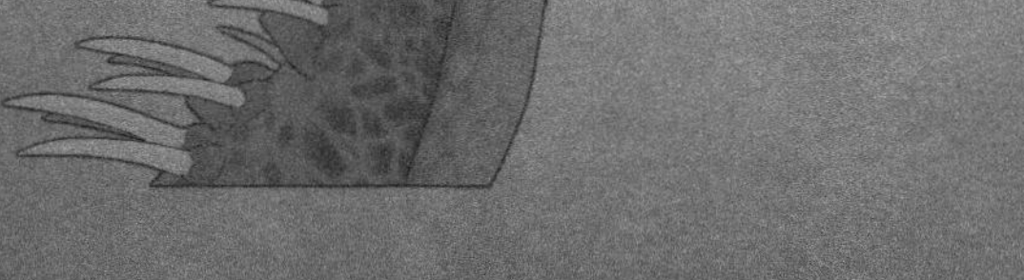

Thank You Once More!

Thank you again to all my Kickstarter backers!

BOADS | ALBERT CUA | BEN HOWARD | KIMBERLY GUEVARRA | KAESON | PAIGE LINO | LEN LUNA | JULIAN MARKER | STUART BUTLER | RYZEN | EMILY P. | CHRIS + KAILIE | MATTHEW CHIN | SEATTLE MIKE | R. SCOTT TYLER | STEPHEN SCOTT | NOEL SCHORNHORST | JUDE COOPER | C. CAROTHERS | STUART TURNBULL | JC ADAMS | ALEXANDER BROWER | AMANDA POGGENBURG | JARROD | STEVEN CASTRO | JOHN H. BOOKWALTER JR. | VASHKALIBROS | STEPHEN B | VICTORIA P | FARIS KARAMAN | BRENT T | STEVEN BRUNWASSER | KAT44 | NIC | TIM SAUKE | PAIGE CRITCHLOW | SARAH KING | KIRA MELHEIM | LEONIDAS BURNS | LARA GRAUERHOLZ-FISHER | GRADY PARROTT | CARISSA KING | NAN | MIKL PICKLE | BIISKIT | ASHLIE MARTIN | TAYLOR HOLDER | KEN HERRINGTON | INODARLZ | LETA BLAKE | C. SPANN | D | MARA | FAISAL K. | JOE CASADONTE & WILL ZANDER | TAL | J RAY | SAYLOR | ALBERTO MOHAMMED-DAWSON | DALE FIELDS | RACHIEL R | JUNIE | BEN | DANIEL FALCO | JOSEPH CONTINELLI | LYNNSIE DIAMOND | MARKUS GEIER | DANI | M. HOLMES | J. B. ZIEGLER | ALYX | PATRICK TIMOTHY | MATTHEW Z | IMANOL ARRIETA | ERIC HENRICKSON | THOBU | VALENTINE | TM | CJ GIBSON | STEPHEN MARTIN | TEPHIC | SUSAN WILSON | MONO | JHMCKEEN | HANNAH C | RYAN | T. J. WILEY | CRISTOV RUSSELL | NICA FLOR | SHAY | CHRIS BURDEN-LOWE | SONG OF INSANITY | ERIK R | DANIELLE GREEN | WILBE | DALE SMITH | IRONREQUIEM | MANUEL Q | MCCREEZO | GRACE NICHOLSON | KATIE GORDON (TOBER2000) | TOMAYTO (HTTPS://TOMAY.TO/)

And To The Royals...

Those who pledged mightily...

Albert Cua

Ben Howard

Boads

Kimberly Guevarra

Kaeson

Paige Lino

Len Luna

Julian Marker

Stuart Butler

Ryzen

Emily P.

THANK YOU FOR READING!

YOU CAN CHECK OUT MORE OF MY LGBTQIA+ COMICS AND ART HERE!

ELEMENT PUBLISHING LLC

- PATREON.COM/MANNYGART
- KO-FI.COM/MANNYGART
- YOUTUBE.COM/@MANNYGART
- INSTAGRAM.COM/MANNYGART
- mannyguevarra.com

www.ingramcontent.com/pod-product-compliance
Lightning Source LLC
LaVergne TN
LVHW070531070526
838199LV00075B/6758